JU[illegible] gets lost

An imprint of Om Books International

Reprinted in 2020

Corporate & Editorial Office
A-12, Sector 64, Noida 201 301
Uttar Pradesh, India
Phone: +91 120 477 4100
Email: editorial@ombooks.com
Website: www.ombooksinternational.com

Sales Office
107, Ansari Road, Darya Ganj
New Delhi 110 002, India
Phone: +91 11 4000 9000
Email: sales@ombooks.com
Website: www.ombooks.com

Content by Sonia Emm

ISBN: 978-93-84625-02-3

Printed in India

10 9 8 7 6 5

JUNO gets lost

I'm all set to read

Paste your photograph here

My name is

Juno is a happy baby kangaroo.

Jill is her loving mamma.

Jill keeps Juno in her pouch.

But Juno wants to go out.

Juno hops out when Jill is asleep.

Z Z Z Z z z z z

But Juno hops so far, she gets lost!

Juno finds a pond.
She meets a frog.

Juno finds a den.
She meets a fox.

Juno sees a tree.
She meets a koala.

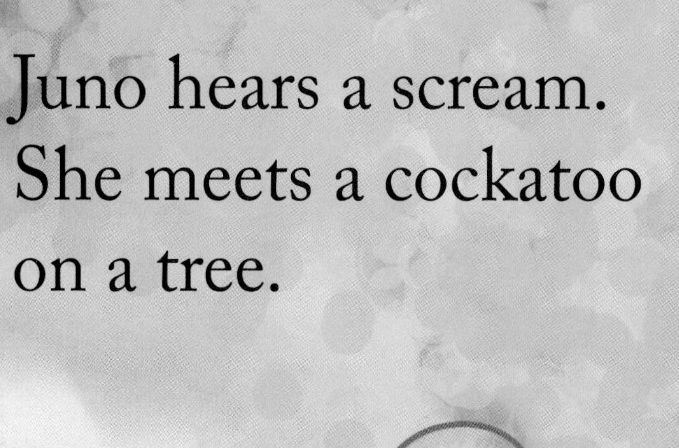

Juno hears a scream.
She meets a cockatoo
on a tree.

Juno sees grass.
She meets an emu.

But where is Jill?
Juno can't see her!

"Juno, turn!"
"It's mamma!" says Jill.

Juno jumps into Jill's pouch.
She falls asleep.

Know your words

Kangaroo - A large Australian mammal that hops from place to place.

Loving - Someone who cares a lot.

Pouch - A little pocket that kangaroos have on their tummies to carry their babies.

Hops - Jumps around, mostly on one foot.

Pond - A tiny body of water, either natural or man-made.

Den - A hollow in a mountain, usually the home of a wild animal.

Koala - A tiny bear with furry ears, found in Australia.

Scream - A loud noise.

Cockatoo - A type of parrot.

Emu - A large bird that cannot fly.